The Call of the Sea

S.F. GOULDESBROUGH

CONTENTS

Chapter One

The sea is quiet this time of night.

Midnight sits heavy over the winding streets, shadowing the cobblestones, hiding the chipped, worn edges of the window frames from sight. The sky is clouded, the moon and stars little more than suggestions through the sea-haze, and as time crawls by, the haar creeps slowly between the houses. Damp beads across the car windscreens, the pub tables, a discarded yellow bucket and spade. Corners of the fishermen's-cottages-turned-holiday-homes are blurred by the fog, obscured in the silence.

The sea laps at the stones of the harbor. The slipway is

lost beneath the glistening dark of the water, and sloshing flicks of spray slap against the lobster pots, the piles of discarded rope, a buoy with a hole slashed in one side. The air tastes of salt, and the stones are slippery underfoot. A lone streetlight stands at the side of the straggling road, but its orange glow barely pierces the fog.

***

SOPHIE WAKES TO THE RUSTLE of the wind around the eaves of her borrowed bedroom.

She lies still for a long moment, not quite sure why she's awake. There's no sound coming from the rest of the house, as far as she can tell. No creak on the stairs, no rumble of conversation from the bedroom next door. The village is a tiny thing, clinging to the side of the cliffs, houses spilling over one another as they pour down to the waterfront, so there are no cars roaring by, no sirens wailing in the darkness, no drunken revelers stumbling home. It's quiet.

Quiet, but not silent.

There's a strange whisper, so soft she barely hears it, skimming the edges of her mind.

She tilts her head in the darkness of the bedroom and frowns as she listens. It hovers in and out of her hearing, coming from faraway, another land, another life, and she thinks there are words, but she can't make out what they're saying. She can't even be sure what language they're spoken in, and she props herself up on her elbow, peers into the shadows as if she'll find her answer there.

She can taste salt, slicked across the back of her tongue.

The whisper rustles louder, like wind in the trees.

"Hello?" she whispers back, but the four walls of the tiny bedroom don't give her an answer.

Driven by an instinct she doesn't understand, she slips out of bed, ducking out from under the top bunk, shucking the patterned sheets in a heap half-on, half-off the mattress. The carpet is thin underfoot and the door creaks on its hinges as it opens, the handle stiff beneath her fingers. She pads down the stairs, avoiding the squeaky floorboards, spiraling down the narrow staircase, and she doesn't know what she's doing, doesn't know where she's going, but before she really has time to think, she's creeping past the sleeping form on the sofa, turning the key in the lock, stepping out of the front door.

The top step is slippery under her bare feet, slick with dark green moss and dripping fog. That should disgust her, she vaguely knows, should send her reeling back inside to fetch thick socks and thicker shoes.

She closes the door behind her with a soft click and moves out into the cobbled street.

The whisper is growing in her mind, still obscure but louder, louder.

This is a dream, she realizes in a more lucid corner of

her brain. It has to be a dream because her reality is not the kind of reality where you are woken by mysterious whisperings in the middle of the night on your girls' weekend away. Too much wine, too much seafood, too many lurid conversations, too much wild imagining. She's dreaming. She's tucked up in that tiny little child-sized bunk bed, fast asleep under the puppy-patterned sheets, snoring faintly, lost in the world inside her head.

Damp cobbles underfoot change to flat stone, smoothed by the endless passage of booted feet.

The slipway stretches down into the fog, its end hidden beneath the slow, susurrating rhythm of the inky water. The edges of the harbor wall are invisible in the creeping haar, and the winding path behind her that leads back to the warmth of the rented cottage is nothing more than a pale blur. The fog whispers against her cheeks, against her bare feet, against her upturned palms, bitterly cold, leaving a delicate lacework of water drops in her hair, loose around her shoulders. There's nothing to be seen of the night sky overhead, no stars, no moon, only the thick heavy blanket of the sea-fog.

The whisper is louder, curling around her heart, rippling down her spine. It isn't words, not quite, or at least it isn't words in any language she speaks, but she understands it, nonetheless.

"Come to me," she echoes, her lips slick with fog-damp.

Moss and dirt are worked between her toes, caught beneath her toenails, smeared across her inner ankles, but that's fine because this is just a dream. She'll wake in the morning, safe in bed, safe and warm and comfortable, and her feet will be clean and dry.

Out in the harbor, hidden by the drifting curtain of the fog, something splashes in the water.

She listens, head tilted to one side, unafraid. There're no following splashes, no sounds of ungainly nighttime swimmers hoisting themselves out of the placid harbor, no voices, no indication at all, in fact, that there is anything other than the foggy silence. She heard it, though, she's certain of that with the uncomplicated certainty of a dream, and so she calls out, "Is someone there?"

Her voice is deadened by the fog, muffled and crumpled. It dies almost immediately. Her heart beats once in the silence, twice, three times.

Another splash cuts through the fog, sharper, more deliberate.

It's an answer, she realizes without even really thinking about it. It's an answer to her question. She asked, *Is someone there?* The answer came back, *Yes.*

She is still strangely calm. "Who are you?" she asks, not bothering to call, not bothering to shout. The words are barely more than thoughts in the foggy night. "Did you bring me here?"

The water is silent, ruffled by the faint breeze, dogged by the pull of the tide, and all of a sudden, the whisper in her mind grows to a scream. She gasps, staggers, catches herself just before she falls—but she can't stop herself from moving forward, stumbling across the stones, picking her way down the slipway between forgotten strands of seaweed and smears of rich green algae. Something sharp pricks the sole of her foot—a bottlecap, maybe, or sea-green broken glass—but she hardly notices, caught up in the power of the command that blares inside her head. *Come to me, come to me.*

She's coming.

This is a dream, it must be.

She staggers to a halt, ankle-deep in the cold harbor water, her chest heaving, fog-wet hair straggling in her eyes, catching at her lips. She can't see the street, can't see the houses, can't see the light of the streetlamp. No, all she can see is the mist all around her and the flat black lap of the water, stretching out in front of her, motionless and featureless in the depths of the night. Her feet slip-slide on the algae-drenched stone. The hem of her pajama bottoms dips in and out of the sea, sticking to her legs, heavy and wet.

All she can hear is the command in her heart and the thumping husk of her own breathing.

She doesn't see anything moving, but one moment she's alone with the fog and the water and the next she is being watched. There's someone standing a little way away from her down the slipway, waist-deep in the water—but no, that doesn't make any sense because the slipway is *steep*, steep enough it would be far too deep for anyone to stand that far out with the tide this far in. They're not swimming, whoever it is, because she can't see legs thrashing beneath the water, and *that* doesn't make any sense, either. The indistinct figure is too far out of the water to just be floating. She looks harder, squinting through the darkness and the fog, and suddenly realizes she's wrong, that there *is* movement beneath the water, it's just that it isn't *legs*.

"Oh, this is *definitely* a dream," she mutters under her breath.

There's a tail moving under the surface, slow and sinuous, barely visible through the dark water. She can't tell how long it is, can't make out the color in this world of black water and white fog, but what she can see is that it's powerful, thickly muscled, and faintly gleaming with the shimmer of silver-gray scales. It's a fish's tail, she's as sure of that as she is of her own name, but it's far too large and— her mind rebels at the thought, tries to shake it off like a dog shaking water from its fur—it's attached to the very human shape still watching her in the distance.

The water is cold against her feet and the wet fabric of her pajamas is clammy and heavy around her ankles. She can feel the beads of dew the fog leaves in her hair, on her skin. There's a sharp pain in the sole of her foot where she stumbled over that bottlecap, that shard of broken glass, that discarded nail or shattered plate.

She looks up to meet dark, black eyes, all pupil, flat and empty, and full of intelligence. Those eyes are watching her, unblinking, steady in their observation, and she can't help but feel that she's being somehow…*assessed.* She's frozen in place, and it's not that she doesn't *want* to move, it's that she tries to raise her hand, but she can't, tries to step back but she can't, tries to turn her head to avoid the flat black of those jet eyes but she *can't.* She's a butterfly on a pin, and all she can do as she is assessed is to assess in return.

The dream-creature is a mermaid. There's no other word for it, really: fish from the waist down, human from the waist up—or at least human*ish.* It's hard to tell in the dim light, but she thinks its skin is gray, the same gray as sealskin and patterned with the same irregular spots. Those dark splotches run down its shoulders and across its chest, fading into the paler flesh of its belly, and she finds herself staring at its flat, taut chest, shadowy in the distance but, well, not quite so indicative of a mer*maid.* The creature has no breasts, no nipples, nothing that would need a seashell bikini or a pair of artfully placed starfish. Instead, its seal-gray torso is streaked with faintly shimmering bioluminescence, veins of blue light that pulse in time with each sweep of its powerful tail, jellyfish-bright in the fog.

Her heart is beating faster in her chest. It isn't quite fear.

For a long time, she can't bring herself to look at the creature's face. She studies the deep-sea lights that burn in its torso, the seal-skin patterning on its shoulders, the silver sheen of its scales beneath the surface of the harbor—but its face, oh, every time she thinks of looking at its face, all she can remember is the *eyes*, black and flat and animal, burning with empty, alien intelligence.

The whisper swells in her head. *Come to me.*

She looks. She can't help herself.

Black, unblinking eyes, so dark they're almost indistinguishable from the darkness at the mer*thing*'s back. A shudder runs down her spine, apprehension, and a strange fascination, because the creature's face is…well, it's *beautiful*. High cheekbones, full lips, long hair as black as its eyes, slicked back with saltwater, threaded through with veins of silver—and those *eyes*, always those eyes, dark and liquid, enticing, inviting.

She takes a breath, so sharp it's almost painful, and steps deeper into the water.

The mermaid smiles, those full lips parting to reveal *teeth*, a mouthful of them, needle-sharp and hungry, bristling around a red, red tongue. That tail swishes through the water, that bioluminescence flares brighter, and all of a sudden, a cold shock of fear floods through her heart. The water, the fog, the night—fuck, this is a *monster*, and it's a dream, it has to be a dream, but it's a dream that has taken a sharp turn into a nightmare.

She turns, lunges for the shore, slips on the algae underfoot and goes to her knees, soaking her pajamas and scuffing her hands on the stone. Those eyes are boring into the back of her neck, she can practically *feel* them, and she chokes out a sob, scrambles to her feet, drags herself back up the slipway as fast as she can. She feels sick, bile thick in her throat, fear a poison in her veins. The fog is so fucking thick around her, smearing across her vision, almost a physical presence, caging her in, pulling her back to the water, to that needle-filled smile, to that *thing* her sleeping mind has conjured out of horror films and nature documentaries and every nameless fear that has ever sniped at her heels in the darkness of the night.

She runs. She doesn't remember much more than that.

Chapter Two

A fist bangs at the door. "You awake, Soph?"

Sophie sits up so quickly she smashes her head into the far-too-low beams of the bunkbed's top bunk. She yelps at the sudden burst of pain, cradles the sore spot, then shouts, "I am *now!*"

There's a familiar snort from outside the door. "Bea says you have to get up," Adam says, sounding distinctly unsympathetic. "You're holding up breakfast."

"Breakfast?" Sophie asks, rubbing at her forehead. "What time is it?"

"Almost ten."

"*Ten?*" She leans out of the too-small bed, scrabbles around on the thin carpet for her watch. Sure enough, in plain white numbers: three minutes to ten. "Fuck," she mutters, squinting up at the window, seeing the unmistakable glare of the late May sun.

"No time for that, I'm hungry," Adam says, as unhelpful as always. "Breakfast is ready. Hurry up or I'll eat all the beans."

"You wouldn't *dare*," she says, gingerly feeling her forehead to make sure she hasn't actually cracked her skull open, but Adam's footsteps are already thudding away down the narrow stairs. She sighs, winces again, then clambers out of bed in the most elegant way you can when the bed is a kid's bunkbed and the duvet is patterned with smiling cartoon dogs.

The moment she stands up, a needle of pain stabs through the sole of her foot. She yelps, hops, then grabs at her toes, turns the bottom of her foot upwards. There's a tiny shard of what looks like bottle glass embedded in her skin. She hisses in pain, fumbles in her weekend bag for a pair of tweezers, yanks the glimmering splinter out, and holds it up to the light.

Her heart thuds in her chest, stuttering and irregular.

"It's nothing." She tosses the glass splinter into the bin and shoves her tweezers away again. "Probably left in the carpet. Fuck knows when this place was last cleaned." She peers at herself in the mirror, rubs perfunctorily at her face, then pulls a jumper on over her pajamas and figures that's presentable enough for a fry up with old friends.

Except the cuffs of her penguin-patterned pajama bottoms are oddly damp.

She frowns, bends down, and plucks at the fabric. It's not just the cuffs, her pajamas are damp up to the knees, already smelling musty like wet laundry left too long in the washing machine. "What the fuck?" she mutters under her breath, grimacing at the smell, then makes the executive decision that she's not going down to breakfast with mysteriously wet pants. She swaps her pajamas for an old pair of leggings, gives her hair a cursory brush—it's stiff and crackling with salt, which is weird—then goes downstairs.

Breakfast is already laid out on the table, sausages and bacon, toast and butter, fried tomatoes, scrambled eggs, and *beans*, blessed beans, magical beans. Sophie sinks into her seat with a groan, pours at least half the beans onto her plate, then digs in.

Vaini slides into the seat next to her, batting Adam away from the butter and spreading it thick across a slice of toast. "Where did you go last night, Soph?" she asks, accepting the pan of eggs from Bea. "You woke me up when you got in. And were you in your *pajamas?*"

Sophie pauses, fork halfway to her mouth. "What?" she asks, face crumpled in confusion.

Vaini stares at her like she's being an idiot. "You came in through the front door at one in the morning," she says, slicing a sausage in half. "Dripping water everywhere. You woke me up and didn't answer when I asked where you'd been."

Sophie blinks, mouth working soundlessly for a moment. "I don't know," she says at last, looking down at the sea of beans on her plate. "I had… weird dreams, though. And my pajamas were wet this morning."

Across the table, Bea cuts a tiny piece off a fried tomato and adds it to the sausage, bacon, toast, egg, and single bean already on her fork. "I didn't think you sleepwalked," she says, then carefully transfers the whole lot to her mouth.

"Is it sleepwalked?" Adam asks, peering into his coffee. "Or sleptwalk? Sleptwalked?"

"Whichever it is, I've never done it before," Sophie says, then plucks at her hair and grimaces. "There's a first time for everything, though. And it would explain my soggy pajamas."

"Mmm, soggy," Adam says.

Sophie frowns at Vaini. "Why were you sleeping on the sofa, anyway?" she asks.

"Vaini nearly died!" Adam says, sounding *far* too cheery about that particular fact.

Sophie blinks again. She's not awake enough for this conversation. "What?"

Vaini grimaces, Adam laughs, and, on the other side of the table, Bea shakes her head as she painstakingly slices the fat off her bacon.

"Turns out I'm allergic to goose down," Vaini says with a sigh. "It's in the pillows. And I didn't know this until I woke up last night and my ears were so swollen, I couldn't get my earrings out." She pokes at her cheek. "My face felt like it was on fire, and I had hives *everywhere*. So I woke Adam up because I thought it would be useful to have a *doctor* on hand."

"I was helpful!" Adam protests. "I gave you drugs!"

"Antihistamines," Vaini fires back. "Which *anyone* could have given me. And then you went straight back to bed while Bea *actually* looked after me. And what was it you said when I told you I was swelling up and in pain?"

Adam grins. "I don't know what you're talking about."

Vaini sighs, gives Sophie an exasperated look. "He said, 'Mmm, splotchy'."

"You *were* splotchy."

Bea rolls her eyes. "You're so helpful."

"Mmm, helpful," Adam says.

"You're not allowed to make that your catchphrase," Bea says.

"Too late," Adam answers with a grin, and somehow manages to make munching on a slice of toast annoying.

"Why didn't you *wake* me?" Sophie exclaims, her

breakfast forgotten. "I can't believe I just slept through all of that!" She reaches out, grips Vaini's wrist. "Are you okay?" She can't resist grinning. "You don't look splotchy any more…"

Vaini gives her a look, then relents. "I'm okay," she says. "No thanks to Doctor McCoy here." She glances at Bea, looking vaguely apologetic. "But I think it might be a good idea to take it easy today? I know we'd planned to go for a walk, but…"

"Eight miles is probably a bit much," Sophie agrees. "I can tell you from past experience, allergic reactions aren't much fun."

Bea sighs, throws her head back melodramatically. "*Fine*," she says. "I spent all that time planning, and you have *one* allergic reaction and want to throw everything out the window?"

"Seems fair, to be honest," Adam remarks. "She did almost die."

"*Adam*," Vaini says.

"What?" Adam asks, spreading his hands. "I'm on your side!"

"I'd prefer it if you weren't," Vaini answers tartly, but there's a smile playing around her lips.

The conversation turns to other things, to their plans for the day, to ice creams in Robin Hood's Bay and jet shopping in Whitby, jokes about Dracula and Heartbeat and the unfortunately named Hole of Horcum. Sophie holds her plate over the table to accept Bea's offered bacon fat, Adam drinks a whole cafetière of the fancy coffee he insisted on bringing all the way from Cornwall, and Vaini shows them all how puffy her face still is by poking herself in the cheek several times.

It's familiar and easy and straightforward, and it's only when Sophie turns the tap in the kitchen sink to wash up that she thinks of her dream again.

It was a dream. It *must* have been a dream.

"Soph?" Vaini asks, piling dirty crockery high on the countertop next to her. "You okay?"

Sophie blinks, grabs Adam's coffee cup, rinses it under the lukewarm water. "Yeah," she says, ignoring the rushing water, ignoring the memory of wet pajamas and damp fog. "Yeah, I'm fine. Just tired." She shrugs, grins. "I guess I sleepwalk now. We'll have to make sure we lock the front door tonight so I don't end up drowning in the harbor."

Bea breezes through the kitchen, only catching the tail end of their conversation. "And nothing of value was lost," she says, grinning.

Sophie flicks soapy water at her, then goes back to washing up.

S.F. Gouldesbrough

Chapter Three

It's a good day.

The four of them roll out of their rented cottage at about eleven-thirty, squinting up at the unexpectedly blue sky. They make the trek up the village's steep and winding streets to the car park at the top of the hill. Staithes is a pretty place, old buildings, softly lapping sea, tiny local shops selling milk and bread and dried-out starfish, and it's already filling with tourists, spilling out of the handful of pubs and restaurants onto the cobbled streets.

They flee from the young families and the elderly couples and spend the day dotting around various beauty spots on the North Yorkshire coast. Sophie chases Vaini with bladderwrack on the beach at Runswick Bay, Bea takes them on a tour of all the places she had arguments with her family as a kid, and Adam entertains himself all evening by insistently heaping logs on the fire in their cottage even when he's told not to.

It's a *good* day.

***

IT'S ALSO A STRANGE DAY.

Sophie doesn't notice it so much that morning, crammed around the worn kitchen table, bumping knees and shoveling beans into her mouth, but there's a strange little scratching at the back of her mind. She passes it off as the echo of last night's wine while they're slogging up the hill to the car, figures it's most likely car sickness when they're driving across the moors, reasons it's too much food too quickly when they stop for lunch.

But it's not.

It's like there's a fishhook caught in the lining of her mind. It tugs at her, uncomfortable, nagging, pulling her back—back to the water, back to the darkness of her dreams.

Which is ridiculous because it *was* just a dream—her subconscious mind processing the events of the day. Just a dream, nothing more.

She stands at the edge of the sea, elbows propped on the

worn, salt-sprayed railing, and stares out across the water. The sky is a dusty kind of gray, shreds of blue creeping through the clouds. The sea below is slate, flecked with white, blank and unimpressive. Behind her, there's a young boy squalling for his mother, a dog yapping in high tones, an old man holding forth on some esoteric topic that whoever he's talking to clearly isn't interested in. The wind curls around her ears, teasing stray hairs free of her ponytail, and every now and then, the odd raindrop splatters against her cheeks.

She watches the sea, watches its restless swell.

Something in her heart tugs, fishhooked, no longer her own.

S.F. Gouldesbrough

Chapter Four

Adam announces he's going to bed a little after half-past eleven, gathers up his Kindle, his mug, and his pocketknife, then disappears up the narrow stairs. The others are still chatting, a meandering conversation about politics and mutual friends, and Sophie has been drifting in and out of for an hour or so. She takes Adam's abrupt departure as an excuse to slink away herself.

"We'll wake you if Vaini tries to die again!" Bea calls, laughter rasping in her voice.

Sophie barely acknowledges the joke.

She slips up to her tiny room, closes the door, crawls

into the bottom bunk. It's cramped and too small even for her, the wall looming at her back, the sheets cheap and infantile against her fingertips, but she doesn't move, doesn't complain, scarcely even breathes.

She's waiting, she realizes. And she knows full well what she's waiting for.

Adam clatters past the bedroom door after a while, humming something tuneless under his breath, and Sophie hears him getting ready for bed, the heavy tread of his footsteps, the creak of the floorboards. It's not long before she hears Vaini's footsteps, too, slower and lighter, the open and close of the bathroom door, the rush of water and the brush of teeth. Bea says something incoherent through the walls, and Vaini laughs softly in response, both of them clearly trying to keep their voices down so they don't disturb Adam or Sophie.

The house settles after a while. There are no footsteps, no rattling pipes, no squeaking door hinges. No conversation, no laughter. The wind whispers around the eaves, rustling with the voices of the dead.

Sophie lies still in the dark, eyes open, unsleeping, and waits.

Chapter Five

The whisper is louder tonight.

34

Chapter Six

She slithers out of bed, still fully dressed, jeans, t-shirt, and jumper, silver studs in her ears, the necklace that was a birthday present from her parents, her watch, her rings. There's an ice cream receipt in one pocket, a discarded safety pin in the other. One sock is patterned with foxes, the other with owls. The door to the bedroom creaks when she opens it, the faintest groan of the hinges, but she pays it no heed, pads downstairs, one hand light on the banister, the other tracing the ugly floral wallpaper.

She hears the call in her mind. It's a siren song if ever

there was.

The front door key sits in the lock. It doesn't make a sound when she turns it.

There's no fog tonight, and the air is clear and sharp with darkness. One illuminated window spills warm light into the cobbled lane but, apart from that glimmer, the tiny village is silent and still. No one is out this late when they could be wrapped up in their blankets and duvets, nestled in front of the embers of the fire, curtains drawn, the outside world forgotten.

She walks down to the waterfront, cobbles hard and dry beneath her socked feet, the smooth concrete a relief when it comes. The water is glassy, a millpond, a blank slate, and as she stands at the top of the slipway, her toes just curling over the edge, she sees it.

It's waiting for her.

The merman, mermaid, mercreature. The monster with flat black eyes, seal-gray skin, electric blue bioluminescence gleaming in the dull light from the streetlamp. Its lips, full and welcoming. Its hair, darker than the night, silver streaked.

It's closer tonight, a little off to the side, and she realizes with a strange twist that it's holding on to the edge of the slipway. Its arms are taut with muscle, stone-steady as it holds itself still, the lash of that powerful tail frozen beneath the water. From where she stands, it could almost be, well, *human*. A wild swimmer out for a midnight dip maybe, wetsuit done up to their chin, reflective strips catching in the faint light.

The mermaid gazes up at her, its eyes luminously dark, and smiles a close-lipped, searching smile.

It's not a wild swimmer.

The whisper swells in her mind, throbbing behind her eyes, snaking cold fingers along her jaw.

Almost without realizing, she steps closer, slipping on the algae underfoot, stepping over broken glass and stray bolts, strands of wiry rope and discarded bottlecaps. The mermaid doesn't move, doesn't make a sound, just watches her stumble closer, ankle-deep in seawater, calf-deep, knee-deep, that enigmatic Mona Lisa smile steady and unwavering on its lips. Closer, closer, and without thinking, she finds herself on her knees, the water up to her waist, her clothes sodden and freezing cold. She's close enough now she can see the details of the dappling across its shoulders, the fainter patterns running up its throat, the soft pulse of the bioluminescent threads in its skin. There are silvery scales scattered across its cheeks, gleaming in the moonlight. Its eyes, oh, its fucking *eyes*.

"What *are* you?" she whispers, her voice sticking in her throat.

The mermaid's smile drops, its lips flattening into a soft line, and slowly, languorously, it extends one hand to her. It could touch her if it wanted to, easily, she's more than close enough for that, but it leaves a gap between them, clear air, empty space. The muscles in its other arm flex as its weight transfers, its tail flicks once, twice to keep it steady, and its fingers unfold one by one, too-long, delicate ghost-gray webbing between the knuckles, each fingertip ending in a pointed, mother-of-pearl nail.

No, not a nail. A *claw*.

She makes a strange noise in the back of her throat, somewhere between a sigh and a moan of fear.

The whispering summons curls around her, soothing her, calming her, *calling* her.

The mermaid is waiting.

"Why me?" she rasps, her voice sounding like it belongs to someone else. The cobbles of the slipway are bony beneath her knees. "Why do you want *me?*"

The black water laps gently around them, dancing with the starlight, rippling with memory, and the mermaid reaches out, runs the back of one finger down her cheek. Its skin is cool and damp, supple like the scales of a fish, and a shudder races through her at its touch. Her heart beats faster, thundering against her ribs, and it's almost like the creature can *hear* it because its gaze flickers down, sharp and hungry. Its hand darts to press flat to her chest, directly above her heart.

The whisper in her mind swells to a *roar*.

Mother-of-pearl claws flash in the moonlight, dip inwards, cut through her clothes and her skin like they're not even there. It's so fast that she doesn't even register the pain for a moment, no, all she does is stare down at the blood as it wells up from the wounds, dark and gleaming in the moonlight, spilling over the monster's claws, staining the yellow wool of her jumper. Oh, *oh*, it hurts, *it fucking hurts*.

She opens her mouth, tries to scream but finds she can't. Her vocal chords are frozen in shock and fear. All she can manage is a halting moan. She feels her eyes bulging, tears sharp, breath heaving, and before she can give in to the paralyzing terror she wrenches herself backwards, pulls away, slips, crashes onto her back, and nearly goes under. She cries out in shock, but it's swallowed by seawater rushing into her mouth. Coughing, choking, she hauls herself up onto hands and knees. Lurching back to the shore, her fingernails break against the cobbles, clothes heavy and sodden, flapping against her skin, dashing saltwater into the gashes on her chest. She moans, drags herself back up to the edge of the harbor, the water behind her, and she's not going to look, she's not going to *fucking look*. She's going straight back to their rented cottage and, in the morning, they're getting out of here. They're getting in the car and they're *leaving*.

She gets to her feet, drenched, one ring missing, jumper bloodstained, the knees of her jeans torn, two fingernails snapped and broken.

Behind her, the water is silent.

She's not going to look.

Somewhere in her half-drowned panic, she lost a sock. There're only the owls now, and as she stares at her one bare foot, she feels the summons throbbing through her brain like a cancer, *come to me, come to me.*

She half-turns, her hands pressed over the growing stain in her chest, and looks.

The ripples from her frantic splashing are already fading, vanishing in the vastness of the ocean, trickling away to flutter against the stones of the breakwater. The night is still once more, serene and peaceful, the moon a silver disc in the sky, stars pricking the darkness—and the mermaid, oh, the fucking mermaid is still there, poised and elegant, taut and sinewy and *watching her*, hand outstretched, mother-of-pearl claws sheened with blood. As she stares, trembling, terrified, sick to her stomach, the mermaid smiles, grins, bares its needle-sharp teeth, and slips silently back into the water.

It leaves nothing in its wake but silence and the whisper that still murmurs in the back of her mind.

Chapter Seven

Sophie stumbles back to the cottage, soaking wet, bloody water dripping between her fingers. She's not sure how she gets to the bathroom without waking everyone else up, but she does, strips off her ruined clothes, dumps them in the bath and clambers into the shower. Under the warm water, she touches the gashes in her chest with shaking fingers, stuffs her fist in her mouth to stifle a sob of pain, bites down on her knuckles so hard they almost bleed, too. She washes the wounds as much as she can because fuck knows what's living on those mother-of-pearl claws, then shakily washes the salt out of her hair, her eyelashes, her skin, scrubs at herself with dragon fruit-scented bodywash until she can't smell the sea anymore.

The dark stretch of the water, the vanishing ripples, the slate-gray ocean beneath the dusty-gray sky.

She gets out of the shower, dries herself with a towel, then swears under her breath when she realizes she's got blood all over it. She balls it up, shoves it into the laundry basket, then wraps herself in another. Gathering up her sodden clothes, she carries them upstairs to her tiny room, dumps them in a corner, and kicks them out of sight. The claw marks are still bleeding, slower, sluggish, and they're clean enough, but she'll need to put some antiseptic on them, maybe some plasters, too. She doesn't exactly carry antiseptic around in her handbag, but Adam's always got a first aid kit with him. Yeah, that'll be where he got Vaini's antihistamines from yesterday. She'll wake him up, get some antiseptic, explain what's happened, and then, at first light, they'll go.

At first light, they'll be gone.

She stands, one hand on the door handle of her tiny, rented room, and doesn't move.

She'll wake her friends. They'll patch her up, they'll look after her, they did it last night with Vaini, they'll do it tonight with her. Antiseptic, antihistamines. They'll go. They'll get out of here, out of this nightmare that leaves her bleeding. Then she'll be safe.

She can't move. She *wants* to move, she really does, but she *can't*. She's frozen, the whisper in her head wrapping around her bones, her muscles, her nerves, and her sinews, coiling around her brainstem, spreading poison through her neurons—and she stands there, her hair dripping into the threadbare carpet, cartoon puppies prancing on the sheets of the bed, and she *can't*.

Tears slip down her cheeks, silent as the sea.

She doesn't know how long she stands there, fingers curled loosely around the doorhandle, trying to turn it, trying so fucking desperately, *fighting*, but when she finally gives up the sky is already lightening outside the narrow, cracked window. The wounds in her chest have stopped bleeding, her hair is mostly dry, and she knows with bitter certainty that she won't sleep even if she gets back into bed. She dresses, dry-eyed, piecing together an outfit from the clothes she has left that are clean, dry, and not stained muddy-brown with her own blood, and does her makeup, smearing more concealer than usual under her tired, tired eyes. Grimacing, she realizes she's missing a ring, covers up the absence by putting on big, gaudy earrings, then picks up her book and goes downstairs, curls up on the sofa and stares at the pages, pretending to read.

She can still hear the whisper.

The electricity of its touch, sliding down her cheek. Those flat black eyes, watching her, holding her. Sleek black hair, ridiculously perfect lips, cheekbones so sharp you could cut yourself.

A spasm of need twists through her, unwanted.

"Soph?" Bea's standing halfway up the stairs, peering at her, bleary-eyed and hair all over the place. She's clearly just got out of bed, and she rubs at her eyes, says with the thick bemusement of the only recently awake, "There's blood all over the towels in the bathroom."

Sophie's heart lurches. "Yeah," she says, slotting the train ticket she's using as a bookmark back into place. "I had a nosebleed last night. Got it all over my clothes and one of the towels in the bathroom. Had to have a shower at like three in the morning."

Bea frowns. "I thought I heard the shower running," she says, rubbing at her face again. "That was you?"

Sophie grins, hoping Bea's far enough away she can't tell how little she means it. "No, it was someone *else* who bled everywhere in the middle of the night."

Bea rubs at her eyes once more, then drops her hands, squints at Sophie. "You don't normally get nosebleeds, do you?" she asks, a little clearer. "That's weird."

Sophie shrugs, goes back to her book. "I don't normally sleepwalk, either," she points out. "Must be something in the air." Inspiration strikes, and she looks up, overdramatic and sharp. "Or maybe it's *Dracula*," she whispers, widening her eyes. "The *dark prince* himself. He's visiting me in the night.

He wants to make me his new bride!"

Bea laughs. "It's the universe telling you that you need to go to the Dracula Experience," she says, turning to pad back up the stairs. "It'll change your *life*."

"It'd better!" Sophie calls after her and feels the lie spread through her like the slow creep of fog on a winter's night.

***

SHE HEARS THE WHISPER COILING at the nape of her neck as she sets the table for breakfast, murmuring in her ear as she listens to Adam and Bea argue about what music to play, sinking its fishhooks into her heart as she waits for her friends to get ready for the day. She hangs back behind the others, dragging her feet up the steep hill out of Staithes, and when the sea rises above the line of the houses, she finds herself staring at it, wanting, *yearning*. The smell of its salt, the cold of its waters. Its darkness, its emptiness.

"Soph, keep up!" Vaini calls, laughter thick in her voice. "I can't deal with these two idiots without you!"

Sophie tears herself away from the sea and jogs to catch up.

S.F. Gouldesbrough

Chapter Eight

They get the bus to Whitby, winding through the little villages and hamlets of North Yorkshire alongside a handful of locals who side-eye them as Bea forgets to adjust her volume and Adam—who lives in *Cornwall*—makes bold proclamations about how he could never live in such an isolated place. The sun is flickering in and out from behind the clouds and the air is heavy with the promise of a storm, but Whitby is still full of tourists, cramming into the arcades, overspilling the streets, crowding the pier and, if they're sensible, avoiding the Dracula Experience. The four of them visit the jet shops, the bookshops, the Abbey, the Abbey museum, the Abbey museum gift-shop, of course, and inevitably find themselves in a brewery, drinking pints under the gathering gloom, laughing, joking, enjoying the company.

Sophie's smile falls every time her friends look away.

The sea flickers in the background of every photo, glimmering in the sinking sun, choppier than it's been so far this weekend.

They get drunk in the afternoon, beers at the brewery followed by far too many bottles of wine at a French bistro that's the only place left with a table. By five they're on the bus home, tipsy and loud, day-trippers exhausted by the sea air, and Sophie finds herself sitting next to Adam, staring past him out of the window watching the sea slip in and out of sight as they rumble along the coast.

Flat black eyes, muscle shifting under smooth gray skin. Mother-of-pearl nails, filed to a point, limned with blood.

"Are you listening to me at all?" Adam asks, amused.

Sophie blinks, shakes herself. "Sorry," she says, grimacing an apology. "I guess I'm just tired."

Adam snorts. "Vaini on Friday night, you last night…" He shakes his head. "I wonder whose body is going to explode tonight."

"It's definitely your turn," Sophie says, propping her head on his shoulder. "And if you keep lighting fires, you won't have to wait for your body to explode—Bea will kill you first."

"Mmm, murder," Adam hums.

Sophie should laugh at that. She doesn't, though, just stares at the back of the seat in front of her, the map of Arriva bus routes across the northwest, feels the rumble of the engine rattle through her, the jolt of Adam's shoulder under her cheek.

***

THE EVENING CLOSES IN.

The storm breaks with a vengeance, rain hammering on the rickety cottage's roof, sheeting down the windows. Lightning flashes the cobbled streets in blue, thunder rumbles overhead like the voice of an angry god. Bea briefly raises the idea of going to the pub across the road, but even she quails in the face of the weather, especially when there's white wine and Peronis in the fridge already.

They drink, they eat oven pizzas, they tear open bags of crisps. They talk.

Or, to be more precise, Bea and Adam and Vaini, *they* talk. Sophie sits in the armchair next to the window, feet pulled up, half-drunk glass of Pinot Grigio getting warm between her hands, and watches the rain, watches it flood down the windowpane, watches it stream down the narrow street, watches the last dregs of the tourists make a break for their cars, bags held above their heads, umbrellas snapped away in the gale, faces caught in expressions of irritation and hysteria. She hears the others say her name occasionally, hears them toss her questions, hears them ask her if she's awake, and she answers when she has to, when there's no other choice. She's not listening.

If she's being honest, she's somewhere else entirely.

The fishhook in her heart is pulling stronger, stronger. She knows she doesn't have the strength to resist.

Chapter Nine

She doesn't remember the others going to bed, doesn't remember the usual spat about who's going to watch the embers of the fire die out, doesn't remember the shuffling around the shared bathroom, the goodnights, the goodbyes. All she remembers is them being there one moment, her friends, loud and raucous, the smell of spilled wine, the snort of laughter, and then a heartbeat later she's alone, the fire dead, the lights off, their shoes piled in a heap, coats shadows of their ghosts on the wall. She's moved, too, wine abandoned, armchair forgotten, standing at the open front door, half out in the lashing storm.

Her hair is already soaked, her cheeks running with rainwater, and there's a throb in her chest that's nothing metaphorical—no, it's the cold and the wet splashing against the wounds dug into her skin above her heart.

Come to me, she hears, so clear it's like someone is standing behind her and speaking in her ear.

She steps out into the night and closes the door.

The storm howls around her; the wind stealing her breath; the lightning illuminating her way to the waterfront in periodic flashes of blue. The streetlights are shorted out, she realizes, their reassuring orange glow nothing more than a memory. At points, the water streaming down the cobbled streets is ankle-deep, rushing over her yellow socks, patterned with tiny, embroidered bees. Her hair lashes her face, tendriled and heavy, and she has to squint against the force of the gale. Her arms are bare, her t-shirt is plastered to her skin, her leggings are stretchy and baggy with the weight of the water.

She stumbles onwards, onwards.

The harbor is a roiling mass of water, the hollow boom of waves striking unmoving stone, froth and foam flying dozens of feet into the air, splattering down across the village. The few small fishing boats at anchor pitch and yaw in the wind, decks sopping, anchor chains taut, fenders flying up with every heave of the waters. It's chaos, all of it, dark and mad, no light, black as pitch, but she walks through the middle of it without hesitation, that fishhook in her heart dragging her onwards.

There's a small, disconnected part of her mind that's fairly sure she's going to die tonight.

There, in the heart of the storm.

The mermaid hangs in the swell, apparently unconcerned by the ravages of the weather. It watches her, bioluminescence flickering through the rain, its eyes the darkest spots in the darkness of the night, and without hesitation extends its hand, long-fingered, mother-of-pearl tipped, webs glimmering with spray. It smiles at her, warm and welcoming, beckons her closer with those sharp, shining claws, full lips hiding needle-sharp teeth. Oh—oh no, no, she doesn't want this.

The whispered call rises in her mind, soft and yielding, the touch of a lover, the comfort of home. It's stronger than she could possibly hope to be.

She steps down onto the slipway, staggers in the wind, rights herself on the green algae slick on the stones underfoot, picks her way forward through the maelstrom. The water rises to her knees, her waist, and she's certain she should have been dragged away by now, dashed against the rocks, carried out to sea, but the path between her and the creature is strangely smooth, rippling with the force of the storm but little more. The water rises higher, her chest, her shoulders, her neck, and all of a sudden, she's swimming. A stuttering breaststroke through the waves, uncoordinated, her legs kicking out of sync with her arms, her body knowing this isn't right even as her mind drives her onward, onward, caught like a fish, hooked and sunk and sinking.

She grabs at the mermaid's hand, cool fingers close around hers, and all the fear vanishes from her heart.

They hang together in the water; the storm raging around them but not touching, not even coming close.

This close, the mermaid is more beautiful than she could have dreamed. The angles of its jaw, the rich darkness of its eyes, the sleek power that lies in every flex of its tail, every ripple of muscle and arch of its neck. She reaches out, helpless to do anything else, trails her fingertips down its cheek, across its lips, down its throat, tracing the darker patterns and the lightning-bright bioluminescence, watching the light flare under her touch. The mermaid watches her, eyes dark, pools of liquid black, and as if in answer it touches her cheek, too, the firm cool of its skin, the chill of its claw, and just as she did before, she shudders, visceral and ripe.

The mermaid smiles, broad and beaming, and settles its hand over her heart.

Lightning cracks across the sky, thunder crashing in its wake.

Come to me, she hears, the words clear and sharp in her mind.

The sea takes her, carries her, pulls her forwards.

As the waves break around them, foam spraying high, wind howling, water surging, she kisses the mermaid, a kiss that isn't tentative, isn't cautious—no, it's the kiss of someone who is so recklessly lost to their love they can't see the horror they are taking into their arms. The mermaid curls around her, one arm around her waist, one hand sinking into her sodden hair, and it kisses her, too, lips cool and salt-sprayed, tongue shockingly warm. It moves against her, the planes of its body firm and languid, the surge of its tail staggeringly powerful in the water, and abruptly she knows that this, *this*, this is where she was always meant to be.

The mermaid's grip on her tightens almost imperceptibly, the whispering call in her mind waxes loud enough to drown out the storm, and they plunge beneath the waves.

The kiss doesn't stop as the water closes over her head. If anything, the deeper they sink, the deeper the kiss gets, passion and need and *heat*, kindling in her belly, a spark of sheer want that overcomes every other instinct. She clutches at the creature in her arms even as she runs out of breath, even as dark spots dance behind her eyes, and there is no panic in her heart, no fear, no horror.

This is right.

This is how it's meant to be.

The mermaid breaks the kiss, deep in the darkness of the waters. They're far from the harbor, now, far from the world, and the only light down here comes from the gleam of the mermaid's bioluminescence. It cants ghostly lines beneath that striking, beautiful face, casts it in a light that's almost sinister, and in the soft illumination of that jellyfish glow, the mermaid bares its teeth, needle-sharp, and settles its mother-of-pearl claws above her heart.

Chapter Ten

Sophie blinks awake, caught, hanging beneath the ocean waves in the grip of a *monster*, a *creature*, a thing of nightmares who is watching her with dead black eyes. Panic shocks through her like lightning— no, oh no, please, this isn't what she wants, *no!* She has to get away; she has to get away from this *thing*. Kicking in its grasp, she twists, pummels her fist against its chest, and opens her mouth to shriek, but it's no use, it's too strong, they're too deep, she has no air left.

She's dying.

Oh *god*, she's going to die.

Sophie screams in the darkness of the sea, the water flooding into her mouth, drowning her as quickly as it silences her, and as searing, scarring horror sweeps over her, the mermaid forces its gleaming claws into her breast and tears out her heart.

Chapter Eleven

"What's that down there?"

Cliff stirs from where he's leaning against the front of the truck, runs a hand through his hair and sniffs sharply as he collects himself. "What's what down where?" he asks, tucking in his shirt, checking that he's zipped up his fly. "What're you talking about?"

Freddie is standing closer to the edge of the overhang, arms folded, peering down at the beach below where they're parked. "There's someone down there," he says, an odd note in his voice. "On the beach. Looks like a woman."

"Didn't think you'd be thinking about *women* right

now." Cliff growls, reaches out, tries to grab Freddie's hand and pull him close. "Not when I've not returned the favor yet."

Freddie knocks his hand away, glances back at him. His lips are bruised from the sea air, from his nervous habit of chewing his bottom lip, and from a spectacular early-morning blowjob. The lust that blazed in his eyes only moments ago is gone. "I'm serious," he says. "There's someone down there, Cliff, and I think she's in trouble." He grimaces. "I left my bloody glasses in the boat again and of course I didn't put my contacts in this morning. Come, take a look?"

Cliff pushes off the truck, grabs a handful of Freddie's arse, and squeezes, probably a bit too rough. "You're lucky you're pretty," he says, kissing him sharply. "Not many other people would get me to go looking for women in the middle of a hook-up."

Freddie's gaze flashes at the phrase *hook-up*, which is fair enough because it's a crass way to describe whatever's been growing between them these past few months—but Cliff doesn't want to have that particular conversation right now. He pushes past, follows Freddie's pointing finger, peers down to the beach below, and regrets both his hastily eaten breakfast and his eyesight, still twenty-twenty in his mid-forties. "Fuck," he breathes, then grabs for Freddie again, gets a handful of his shirt, holds on tight. "You got your phone?"

"Yeah," Freddie says warily. "Yeah, why?"

"Call the police," Cliff says, not letting go, not *ever* letting go. "That woman, Fred, she's not in trouble. She's *dead.*"

Freddie goes white and fumbles his phone out of his pocket.

***

THE NINE-NINE-NINE OPERATOR warns them it'll take an hour or so for the police to show up and somehow it doesn't feel right to leave the poor girl's corpse abandoned on the beach like that, so they stay.

There's an old tarp in the back of the truck that Cliff fetches before Freddie stops him and points out that they probably shouldn't disturb the body, which is a good point, but still doesn't feel *right*. He grumbles to himself about police procedure shows as he takes the tarp back to the truck, leaving the dead girl with Freddie—who's still looking a little green around the edges from his initial bout of vomiting. Cliff can't exactly blame him: the gaping hole in the girl's chest makes his stomach clench in warning every time he thinks about it.

When the police car finally pulls up next to the truck up on the overhang, Cliff waves them down, then winces as he sees who it is. "Shit," he mutters under his breath, taking a deliberate step away from Freddie. "It had to be Roy, didn't it?"

Freddie squints at him, the morning sunlight glancing through his thick blond hair. "Roy?" he asks, his voice tight. "As in, *Roy*? Your *cousin* Roy?"

Cliff nods tightly.

Roy's expression is shuttered as he comes down the path to the beach, thumbs tucked in his vest, gaze flickering between Cliff and Freddie. "Cliff," he greets as a pair of yawning crime scene techs pick their way past. "And you are?"

"Fred Sanders," Freddie answers, arms folded across his stomach, still looking like he might vomit any moment.

"He works with me," Cliff says before Roy can ask anything else. There's a challenge in his voice he can't quite tamp down, a challenge that, after all this time, he doesn't *want* to tamp down. "On the boats in Whitby. Been with us six months or so."

Roy eyes him. "What were you two doing out here this early?" he asks, clearly ignoring everything Cliff just said. "Not the kind of place I'd expect to find a man like you." He glances at Freddie, gaze cold. "The kid, maybe. Not you, Cliff. Didn't take you for *that* kind of fella."

Cliff squares his shoulders, firms his jaw. "And what kind would that be?" he asks, taking a step forward, shielding Freddie with his body if he has to. "You got something you want to say to me, Roy? Say it."

Roy shrugs, untucks his thumb from his vest and reaches for his notebook. "Just making conversation," he says, flipping the notebook open to a fresh page. "I'll need to take your details, gents. Cliff Harper, I know you well enough already. Fred Sanders, was it? I'll need an address and a phone number. We'll probably have some follow-up questions down the line."

Freddie glances at Cliff, his eyes troubled, but reels off his details, anyway.

***

THEY DON'T LINGER LONG AFTER that.

A white tent has gone up around the girl's body, her gutted corpse thankfully hidden from view, but Cliff knows he's going to be seeing *that* particular image in his nightmares for a fair while. More pressing is the fact that he's pretty sure he's about to be outed to his whole bloody family because of Roy fucking Barker, and that's what he's thinking about as he trudges back up the path to where they left the truck. He slips behind the wheel, fishes his keys out of his pocket and shoves them into the ignition, turns the engine on, then stops abruptly before he puts her in gear.

Freddie's still standing out on the overhang, staring out at the sea.

Cliff rolls down the window, leans out. "Forget him,

Freddie," he says, gruffer than he means. "It doesn't matter. We'll work it out."

Freddie doesn't move. As a matter of fact, he doesn't even seem to have heard.

Cliff frowns, clambers out of the truck. "Fred?" he asks. "You hear me?" He touches Freddie's arm, wants to take his hand but is acutely aware of his cousin down below, staring up at them, lip curled in a sneer.

Freddie stirs at his touch, his expression strangely faraway. "Cliff?" he asks, his voice hoarse, then clears his throat, blinks. "Sorry, I didn't hear that. I was miles away."

"Well, you'd best get back here quickly," Cliff says, tugging him away from the edge of the overhang. "We're already late. Not sure how forgiving Gary's gonna be, even when we tell him about the dead girl."

Freddie sways back towards the overhang, towards the beach, towards the sea. "I just…" His forehead furrows, and even as Cliff is pulling him back to the truck, he looks back over his shoulder, gaze lingering. "Can you hear that?"

Cliff can hear the conversation of the techs, the rustle of the wind through the sedge grass, the rasp of his own footsteps against the sandy soil. "Hear what?"

Freddie doesn't answer, still gazing at the sea, broad and blue-gray the morning after last night's storm. Tiny white crests foam along the rolling waves, seagulls swoop and holler in the breeze, and out in the depths, further than

Freddie can see without his bloody glasses, Cliff can just about make out what looks like the head of a seal. It slips beneath the waves after only a second or two, vanishing into the dark water.

Cliff tightens his grip on Freddie's arm, shakes him lightly. "Hear *what*, Fred?" he repeats.

Freddie doesn't look at him. "Whispering," he says as the sea rumbles endlessly against the shore, his eyes glassy, his voice faraway. "I can hear someone whispering."

S.F. Gouldesbrough

S.F. Gouldesbrough writes science fiction, fantasy, and horror in the rainy north of England. She wrote her PhD on science fiction and classical literature at the University of Oxford, and now works as a librarian.

Macabre Minima

Macabre Minima is a small, independent publisher based in Melbourne, Australia. Founded in 2018, our aim has always been to champion emerging authors from all around the globe and offer opportunities for them to participate in speculative fiction and horror short story anthologies.

S.F. Gouldesbrough

72

The Call of the Sea

Coming Soon

Developmental

by Emily Fox

76

In the weeks after Rudy was born, I lay awake, drenched in postpartum sweat, hearing the howling of wolves in my ears. Night after night, they circle closer to the broken, white pickets surrounding our chipped-paint lavender cottage. The sounds of their teeth snapping outside the window leave me gasping and running to his bassinet. I nurse him most nights, clutching his body to my breast in tight-fisted desperation, staring at the shadowed backyard.

I didn't tell Riya immediately about the dark, canine shadows that call out to me from just beyond the yard. They stay close to the fence line, skulking and amorphous. It is easy to write them off as a trick of the eye—sleep deprivation demons of the newly minted mother—until the streetlights catch the metal glint in their eyes. A flash of silver iris like a lighthouse bulb spinning before blinking out into the dark, churning sea.

I think about my mother and the days before she left us at my grandmother's house and didn't come back for a very long time. I think about the way she pulled the drywall off in neat chunks, meticulously checking each piece as if she were a jeweler spying for imperfections, turning each section with careful precision before placing it in a crumpled Revco shopping bag.

"This is where they put the bugs," she would tell us when we asked her what she was doing. "That's how they can hear you, everything you say, everything you do." Her eyes shone with the glittering emerald of what I now know was madness. She grabbed my shoulder and pulled me close, her metallic breath burning my face, tinged with Merit Ultra-Lights and Midwest methamphetamine. "I will never let them come for us, baby".

Thinking she was talking about real bugs, I nodded my head in agreement. I hated the bugs in our apartment and the way they would run for the corners when you flipped on the lights. I hated how they made my little sister cry in the dark when they ran across her face while she tried to sleep, their legs like dirty eyelashes stuck to her skin.

My mother's eyes were fire those nights, watching the corners for things we could not see. I wonder if she were here, could she see the wolves too, running suicides back and forth just beyond the fence? I watch the walls of Rudy's nursery, willing myself not to pick at the cracks in the plaster.

Riya offers to stay up with the baby, but I won't let her. I am determined to be all the things my mother wasn't—all the things my sister would never get to be. In our marriage, I am the one prone to emotional peaks and valleys, while she tends toward dogged practicality. A chemical engineer who had risen quickly in her career due to her precise and pragmatic mind, Riya is my true north when the compass went spinning and Rudy had spun the compass. No one can truly prepare you for how much parenthood changes the direction of your life, but Riya believed in me. She believed me in a way that only people who have never watched their mother pick the walls apart can believe in you. However, I know what happens to mothers who see things that no one else can see. They go far away, and they never come back.

These days, the wolves and I keep our own company.